To Percy L. Knight

Text and Illustrations Copyright © 1986 by Helena Clare Pittman.

Library of Congress Cataloging-in-Publication Data

Pittman, Helena Clare.
  Martha and the nightbird.

Summary:
A beautiful Nightbird takes Martha on a
magical ride through the night skies.
[1. Birds — Fiction. 2. Night — Fiction. 3. Fantasy] I. Title.
PZ7.P689Mar   1986   [E]   86-6810

ISBN: 0-89845-491-3
Published by Caedmon, New York
Printed in Hong Kong   First Edition
10 9 8 7 6 5 4 3 2 1

Martha and the Nightbird

Written and Illustrated
by Helena Clare Pittman

Caedmon

A Nightbird calls in the darkness.

The notes ride on the moonlight
into the room where Martha is sleeping.

In and out of her dream weaves his song,
until Martha pulls herself up
by the feathers of his neck,

they go,

up

up,

up,

and

to the top of the sky —
for the moon and stars to light their way . . .

over the countryside,
where a train is making its way
through the hills to the station,
carrying mail, and milk,
and passengers tired from the long night's ride.

Martha's joyful shouts
ring on the night air over the harbor,
where shoremen are unloading cargoes
that have crossed the ocean,
and the shimmering
bay has a dancing moon of its own.

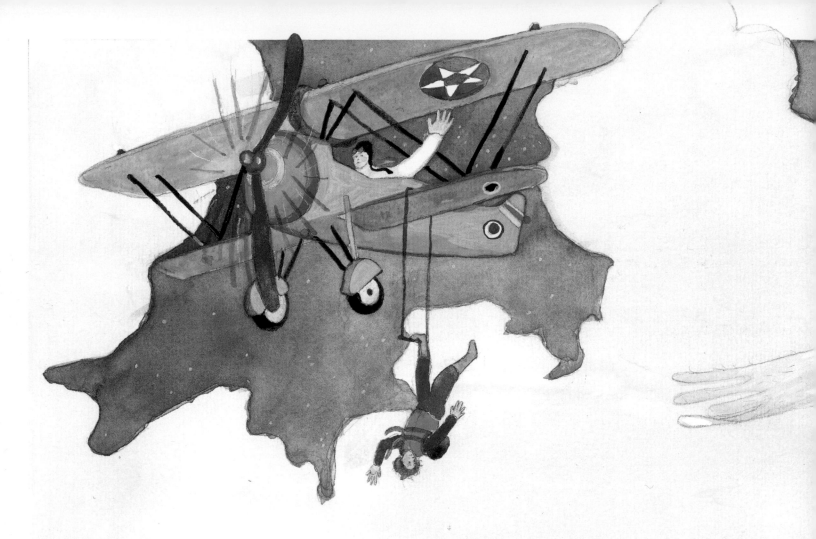

Above the airport,
they race with a plane

and watch until its winking lights
disappear into the deep purple sky.

They glide over the park,
where dogs are having a midnight snack,
cats are singing to the moon,
and pigeons are nesting in the eaves
of the zoo buildings.

Just Martha and that bird
circling a radio station
playing music through the night —

and a house where a man is awake, remembering.

Martha and the Nightbird, sailing over the empty streets,

passing above a field where a flock of geese
is preparing for a long journey,

above treetops and houses

where a night watchman is arriving home,
and a poet rises in the dawn to shape the morning sounds
into words with her pen.

Suddenly a hundred birds send their cries
into the breaking day,

where they mingle with the Nightbird's song
and Martha's breathless laughter.

The moon and stars scatter.
Back they go to the top of the sky.
Then down,
        down,
            down
                drifts Martha,
                    holding tight to the Nightbird's wings.

Down,
   down,
      down on the notes
        of his song

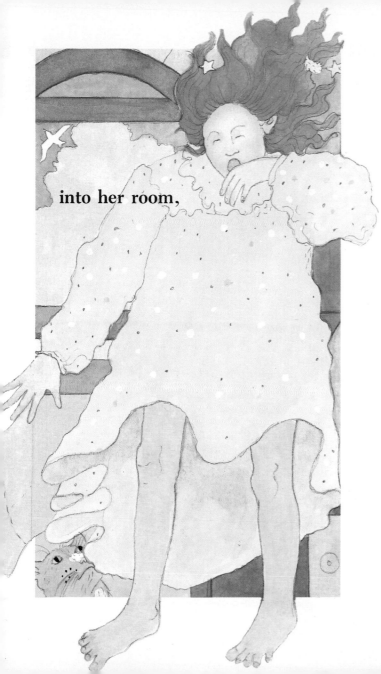

into her room,

and into her dream,
where the melody
mixes with

"MARTHA!"

Martha's toes are frosty,
and there are feathers in her hair.